The Teeth of the Comb

ALSO BY OSAMA ALOMAR
from New Directions

Fullblood Arabian

Osama Alomar

THE TEETH
OF THE COMB

and other stories

*Translated from the Arabic
by C. J. Collins with the author*

A NEW DIRECTIONS PAPERBOOK ORIGINAL

Manufactured in the United States of America
New Directions Books are printed on acid-free paper
First published in 2017 as New Directions Paperbook 1370

Library of Congress Cataloging-in-Publication Data
Names: Alomar, Osama, 1968– author translator. | Collins, C. J., 1977– translator.
Title: The teeth of the comb & other stories / by Osama Alomar ;
translated by Osama Alomar and C. J. Collins.
Description: New York : New Directions, 2017.
Identifiers: LCCN 2016039664 | ISBN 9780811226073 (alk. paper)
Classification: LCC PJ7914.L586 A2 2017 | DDC 892.7/37—dc23
LC record available at https://lccn.loc.gov/2016039664

10 9 8 7 6 5 4 3 2 1

New Directions Books are published for James Laughlin
by New Directions Publishing Corporation
80 Eighth Avenue, New York 10011

Because a mother is a universe in which creatures don't get lost,
I dedicate this book to my universe

لأن الأمّ هي كونٌ لا يضيع فيه مخلوق .. أهدي هذا الكتاب الى كوني

The Teeth of the Comb

Journey of Life

I WALKED THROUGH crowds of people, looking for him among the thousands ... the millions, prospecting for him ... crossing mountains and valleys, seas, and plains, walking purposefully in crowded areas, carrying with me compasses and dozens of maps. I looked in all directions. Sweat poured from me in profusion. Worry ate at me. I continued on my path toward the north. The cold nearly killed me ... oh god ... where is he? ... where is he? I screamed as loud as I could ... Question marks called out from everywhere. I asked passersby about him. They looked at me with incomprehension. I walked among humans, calling him with all my strength, "Where are you, my beloved? I beg you: show me your face."

Only indifference and the dull rhythm of life answered me.

Little by little I began to advance in age ... I lost most of my weight. My legs became much weaker than before. I bought a cane and continued the journey I had started years before, searching for him. I reached places that ghosts had never reached. I rested in caves made from rock and fear. I escaped from wild beasts who nearly made me their poor meal. I crossed the globe, east and west ... north and south ... my stumbling steps mixed with my stumbling luck. I fell ... With the enthusiasm of youth, my old age raised a flag of victory over my body. My head bled. I lifted it very slowly, fighting the hand of exhaustion that tried to push it down. I looked toward the far horizon—maybe I would glimpse a trace of him. A swamp of desperation caressed the shores of a glistening lake of hope, trying to swallow it. But with all my strength I stretched my feeble hands into my past and snatched what I could from the strength of my youth.

I stood on my shaking legs and continued my journey, searching for humanity until the last moment.

Bitter Cold

BECAUSE HE HAD spent long years luxuriating in the warm paradise of his family home, he fell gravely ill and nearly died in society's bitter cold.

The Knife

HE WAS BORN with a silver knife in his mouth. And he was its first victim.

Freedom of Expression

THE GOVERNMENT ISSUED a decree guaranteeing citizens the right to freedom of facial expression. It was considered a big step forward, especially since many countries had banned this form of expression entirely. Millions of citizens took to the streets in huge demonstrations of support for this great and unprecedented victory for democracy. They smiled widely as they marched, their faces grotesque masks of joy.

Swamp

I TURNED INTO a swamp of inactivity, and because of this no one was able to see the gems in my depths.

Compression

AKRAM CURSED THE day he compressed his age from seventy down to twenty, because the impotence of childhood became mixed up with the impotence of old age. Painful memories intermingled with happy ones, success united with failure, and marriage united with divorce. Laughter mixed with tears, and friends and enemies were fused in the same melting pot. The borders between positives and negatives disappeared. The magical influence of time to heal pains and calamities vanished into nothingness. And so, deciding to enjoy his true age, Akram undid the compression of time.

On Top of the Pyramid

AN ENORMOUS GARBAGE bag, seeing the social pyramid shimmering in the sunlight, wanted to reach the top. He made great attempts to climb up, but every time he would slide back down. After many failed attempts, his efforts finally brought success. He sat regally at the top of the pyramid out of breath from both fatigue and the intoxicating joy of victory. The thrill of his accomplishment caused him to forget the suffering he had endured.

But within moments the apex of the pyramid had pierced a hole in the bag. Soiled water mixed with garbage poured down the four sides until the whole structure was covered in a monstrous pile of slimy debris whose hateful smells permeated even distant places.

Don't Give Up the Fight

WHILE CAVORTING IN a field, the wild horse felt overjoyed to see a water hose flailing in all directions, water spraying from it fearsomely as a farmer tried in vain to grab hold of it. The horse shouted as loud as he could, encouraging the hose, "Don't give up the fight!"

The hose answered him enthusiastically, "Right on, my friend!"

The Sold Nations

WHEN THE TRANSACTION was complete, the merchant put the money in his pocket. One of the bills said to her colleague with annoyance, "I'm tired of moving from hand to hand so easily. We need stability so badly!"

Her colleague answered her with sadness, "We were born for this end my dear"; she sighed and then resumed, "We are like nations that have been sold, imprinted with thousands of fingerprints, and crammed into thousands of pockets until they are in tatters."

Minutes later, after another transaction, the merchant pulled one of the bills from his pocket hurriedly. She didn't even have enough time to say good-bye to her colleague before she settled into a cold wallet.

The Diamond and the Coal

TWO YOUNG MEN, one rich and one poor, were discussing their respective futures. The rich one put a big diamond down on the table and said excitedly, "This is my future."

The poor one put a piece of coal on the table and said sadly, "This is mine."

Then each one went on his way. But the diamond felt a longing for her origins and drew close to the piece of coal and hugged her tightly.

Psychological Barrier

I CLIMBED UP the psychological barrier that separated me from a high functionary, but I fell back and broke my leg. He looked over the barrier at me, and after kicking my dignity with feet of insults, he threw me in prison. The next day he surrounded his palace with psychological electric fences!

Descender!

THE ELEVATOR THAT was going up to the top floor looked at his colleague who was going down to the lowest and called to him disdainfully, "You descender!"

But after a while the roles were reversed and so were the names.

Closing the Blinds

WHEN I CLOSED the thick blinds on the veranda so that my neighbors couldn't see my four wives and my young daughters, I discovered with great happiness that this was a perfect way to observe other men's wives and their young daughters!

Insults

WALKING OUT OF my house on the way to the market, I thought I heard each step of the staircase insulting the one below him. When I listened more carefully, I found it was my shoes expressing their disdain for each step, starting from the top!

Bag of the Nation

I TOOK THE big bag that I had inherited from my grandfather down from the attic. It was brightly colored like a storm of rainbows. I hoisted it onto my back and went out into the street. I closed my eyes and began to choose samples at random from everything that was inside: humans and stones and dust and flowers and the wind and the past and the present and the future.

I carried the heavy bag on my back and set off on a far-ranging journey around the world, proudly carrying the overflowing wonders of my nation's genius.

As soon as I arrived in the first of the many countries I had decided to visit, I headed toward the public square and stood in the middle, shouting out as loud as I could, "Ladies and Gentlemen ... Ladies and Gentlemen! I have come to you from a faraway country carrying roses and flowers ... concepts and creativity ... a history glorious with the colors of spring, as well as a future that desires to stand humbly before my nation's lofty gate."

The magnetism of my shouting drew in all sorts of people from the arteries that opened onto the square until they became a thick crowd. Voices quickly rose: "Come on, stranger … show us what you have … show us the wonders and the creativity of your country."

I took the heavy bag off my back, sweat pouring off me, and combed the crowd with a look full of confidence. I undid the mouth of the bag and opened it wide, but when I did, an atomic irony exploded, blowing me into the air, then dropping me to the ground. Everyone burst out laughing. Some of the men even rolled on the ground clutching their stomachs. But the women and the children looked at me with disgust. Many turned their heads away.

The surprise shook me like an earthquake … my spirit filled with cracks. One of the people from the crowd came toward me and gave me a small mirror, then turned and went away laughing. I looked in the mirror. The horror! My face had been terrifyingly disfigured. As for my country's reputation, it had suffered degradations such as it would not recover from for tens if not hundreds of years.

"Oh my country … what did you do to me … what did I do to you?"

I cast my tearful gaze about the square that was emptied of even the breeze. I tried to get up slowly, propping myself up on my broken spirit, but I immediately fell back down. I repeated the effort many times. Finally I succeeded. My thighs trembled as if the shards of my self-confidence had joined together there. I looked at the charred bag of the nation. I looked at the effects of the atomic irony explosion. Tears fell thickly from my eyes, trying to make their way through the peaks and crags of my ravaged face. I picked up the bag and threw it into the sea and wandered off not knowing where.

They Stick Out Their Tongues at Me!

WHEN I WAS young I would laugh at old people all the time. Now I am old and the memories of my youth have begun to stick out their tongues at me and dance their eyebrows, saying, "Hey old man!"

Bowed Heads

AN EMPTY EAR of wheat looked across the field to a crowd standing in a line along the straight road. Their heads were bent before their tyrant leader. The empty ear said sadly to herself, "How lucky are these humans. Their heads are bowed with the blessing of fullness!"

The Beauty of Youth

IN HER YOUTH she was wrapped up in the spiderweb of people's gazes. But when she grew old the web tore of its own accord.

Love Letter

DEAR MINERVA:

I don't know how it happened. All I know is that the flowers of my feelings blossomed in the spring of your beauty with its powers of birth and its shining radiance in all parts of the globe all at once. Do you remember how we met each other at a performance of *Waiting for Godot?* I was holding the playbill. You were carrying a stack of books. You seemed like a serious university student. I didn't feel like taking the initiative to talk to you, despite your captivating beauty. But, when you sat next to me by total coincidence just before the performance began, and asked in a voice made of silk if you could take a look at my playbill, I felt the frost begin to turn into drops of dew at the dawn of something mysterious and enchanting. I was annoyed by the beating of my heart, which seemed like the heart of a teenage boy speaking to a girl for the first time in his life: Be quiet, heart … don't expose my emotions before the throne of beauty … Be quiet, heart … I won't let the hot coals of your crazy pulsing or the lava of your volcanoes block my way to this charming woman!

That night I felt like I would finally get out of the pit of my loneliness full of gloomy insects and poisonous creeping reptiles. When you talked about Beckett with enthusiasm, I felt a hidden happiness … I felt a thin, shining thread among many other threads begin to join us together. When you spoke about literature, I climbed on board a mythical ship making its way on a magic ocean always shining under the spring sun.

We started going to films and the theater together. Sometimes you would be more than an hour late for our meetings, provoking in me anger mixed with worry. You would offer excuses and I would always forgive you because the sight of you coming from far away seemed to me like a long-awaited dawn.

When you talked, I couldn't concentrate on your words because I would get lost in the rich forests of your green eyes, dazzled by their enchanting creatures.

Little by little, I understood that our souls had become two harmonious melodies inside a single song.

After six months of meeting regularly, we decided to get engaged. I was possessed by a wonderful feeling that I had never felt before. I bought a beautiful bouquet of flowers and put on my best clothes. I went to your family's house, propelled by an enormous burst of energy, even though I knew that you had had serious disagreements with your mother.

I remember how she opened the door for me with a coldness that let something of winter shiver into my soul. I remember how your father remained throughout the meeting not saying a word, sipping his tea in little sips. When your mother found out that I was a third-level government functionary, her face became an arctic frown blowing an icy wind around me. She asked me in a strong voice, "Do you think that you will be able to provide for my daughter with your meager salary?" She refused me, because for the crime of poverty the court of society had sentenced me to hard labor. After a short conversation where we couldn't hear each other at all, I started shivering from the terrible cold. As I went down the steps of your house, I could hear you and her fighting. You were a spring breeze swallowed within seconds by winter's savagery.

The strange thing was that our meetings became more intimate and more tender after that visit …. How much I love you … you who presses my heart in the contractions of your pupils!

But a new idea began to obsess me day and night: emigration—moving to a very faraway place. This thought threw me into a bitter struggle with the weight of your love. What cut me most was your total rejection of the idea.

In the end reason won a bloody battle over the heart.

Just before I climbed the steps up to the airplane, you sent me a last text message. It said, "Wherever you go … my spirit will be with you, guarding you and protecting you from bad people."

Since that day, my soul is more filled with yours than ever before.

We stayed in constant communication by e-mail. I told you about my exile, and you told me about yours, at home among the people closest to you. Thousands of miles separate us, but the scent of your perfume fills the huge city where I live. The rich forests of your green eyes surround me with their magic.

When the revolution began, my heart lit up with a fire unlike any I had known before … a special kind of fire, a revolution against oppression and slavery …. I swam in an ocean of happiness, drinking its strong, sweet water. Now the flowers of freedom had finally blossomed in the minds and hearts of the people.

But little by little the revolution against tyranny and oppression became something else … The tyrant who had been sleeping in the depths of the ordinary citizen began to wake up, baring his fangs. The country entered through the widest gate the hell of sectarian and civil war. The nation's severed limbs were mixed up with the severed limbs and heads of its humans. I watched the events, not believing what was happening. When the situation had gone so far down the road of destructive chaos and insanity, I came to understand that the enslavement of humans to deadly and destructive notions and ideas is far more dangerous than the enslavement of humans to other humans, and the road to the paradise of freedom and human dignity is spread with tongues of hell.

Oh my love ... since news from you stopped coming I am looking for you everywhere, asking our common friends ... in vain. In what direction have the claws of insane war thrown you? I watch the great ship of humanity steered by oppression, that terrifying black savagery that never gets tired .... The world has enough room for all the dead ... but not for all the living. Scientific progress serves human backwardness. High technology is in the hands of cavemen.

I look for you everywhere. I look for my soul. I will send you this message for the hundredth time ... Should I send it by mail or e-mail ... or put it in a bottle and throw it into the sea? All I know is that I will continue writing my letters to you until I find my soul.

A Taste

SATAN TASTED WITH the tip of his finger a very tiny amount of human hatred. It poisoned him and he died right away.

The Smells

THE YOUNG MAN returned from a month-long voyage of discovery in the forest—he had been searching for new and exciting things. Back inside his house, he let out a long sigh pregnant with deep exhaustion. He took off his shoes and socks and clothes, and lay down on the couch, falling within moments into a deep sleep.

Strong smells from his feet permeated the room. Feeling great embarrassment, the two feet looked enviously at the young man's hands and asked them, "Why don't repulsive smells emanate from you like they do from us?" The hands answered in a loud voice, "Because we are always open to others and absolutely refuse to be closed in on ourselves."

Nests

THE BIRD RESTED in his nest after hours of flight and looked down at the homeless people in the park, sleeping on the pavement despite the bitter cold.

"It's strange and unfortunate," he said, "that so many humans don't have a nest to shelter them and drive away the dangers of the outside world. I never in my life saw a bird that didn't have a nest to hold him and his young in a warm embrace. The life of these creatures must be marked by some great flaw."

He wrapped his chicks in his wings with tenderness and fell into a deep sleep.

Quicksand

"IT'S RARE THAT anyone gets away from me," the quicksand said in a voice filled with confidence.

But the quicksands of life answered her scornfully, saying, "How many people keep flailing and thrashing in me all through their life, and they neither get away nor drown entirely!"

The Feather and the Wind

THE FEATHER SAID to the wind in a slain voice, "What's this tyranny?"

The wind answered her, "What's this weakness?"

Black Holes

SHE LOVED HIM intensely but her love was not reciprocated. She tried hard to infiltrate his heartbeats ... but without success. And so her soul filled with black holes that prevented her inner light from escaping. Stricken and emotionally starved, she began to swallow the light of any love that passed near her. Little by little she became a universe of light that no one could see.

Free Elections

WHEN THE SLAVES reelected their executioner entirely of their own accord and without any pressure from anyone, I understood that it was still very early to be talking about democracy and human dignity.

Warm and Cold

WHEN THE CAPTIVATING warmth of love penetrated me, my spirit expanded infinitely, embracing and drawing in the greatest number of souls. But when the bitter cold of hatred invaded it, my spirit contracted to the point where it could not even contain itself.

Humility and Arrogance

WHEN I WAS humble, I thought I was a river flowing toward the sea. Becoming arrogant, I grew strongly convinced that the opposite was true.

Circumstances

SEEING THE TREES growing straight and vertical on the slope of the mountain, I realized that it is completely natural to remain standing upright even when we grow out of deeply sloping circumstances.

The Emerald

THE EMERALD NECKLACE was eaten with envy over his mistress's green eyes, and he nearly died of jealous rage when he saw them shining with pearly tears over her husband's death.

The Light of Hope

HE DIDN'T KNOW how he had arrived in that strange place. All he knew was that he had woken up and found himself in a dark and very narrow tunnel that seemed to have no end. He curled himself into a ball, shivering from fear and cold, but then began to feel around the walls of the tunnel. They were made of iron. Like beggars debilitated by hunger looking for a crust of bread in the garbage, his eyes began to search for a ray of light to bring hope into his trembling heart.

"What brought me here? Who threw me in this cold, iron coffin? Where is my family? Where are my wife and children?"

The thunder and lightning of questions—a downpour of poisoned nails—rained down on his soul. He knocked on the walls of the tunnel, hoping that someone might notice and come to save him from that miserable place. He kept knocking for a long time until he felt that his knuckles were about to break. He continued his work with his other hand, but with no result. No one answered him except an eerie, tight-lipped silence.

He became easy prey for all sorts of black thought-streams that deafened him with their hissing. He curled into himself more tightly than before, shivering from hunger and cold and resignation. He no longer knew how long he had spent in that miserable place, "Three days ... a week ... a month? ... Ah, what is harder than not knowing the age of our sadness?"

The biggest question came back to scream inside him, "What brought me here?"

Then suddenly, as if by divine miracle, a very thin sliver of light appeared at the end of the tunnel. He sprang into alertness and rubbed his eyes. "It's really light ... light!" He felt like crying, but he controlled himself. As he watched the light grow in strength and clarity, he gathered up the sputtering candle of his power. Energy spread through him. He didn't know where it came from, but he began to crawl with eager determination toward the light, which had become dazzling.

As soon as he got to the end of the tunnel, he fearlessly pushed his head and hands and then his whole body out of the opening.

When he landed on the ground, he lifted his dusty head very slowly. The sun was at its zenith. He looked up with squinting eyes at the tunnel he had come from to see that it was the barrel of a cannon being raised upward in preparation for firing.

Insult

AS YOUTH HANDED over a woman of amazing beauty to Old Age, he said, "Be nice to her. Don't insult her beauty."

Old Age answered him with anger, "Better to insult her than to insult myself!"

The Waist and the Mind

THE DANCER SHOOK her waist, and showers of money rained down on her, which her fans and followers gathered up and put in her golden purse.

The great thinker shook his head, and jewels of ideas fell from it, which the people crushed underfoot without even feeling them.

The Earthquake

THE UNEMPLOYED YOUNG man suffered a psychological earthquake with a magnitude of 8 on the Richter scale. It almost completely destroyed the city in which he lived. The loss of human life was horrifying.

The authorities were astounded at this unprecedented disaster. They undertook to rebuild the structures of the city in a different form, reinforcing them with materials resistant to human earthquakes. Unemployed young men began to be regarded with utmost seriousness and caution. Unemployment was eradicated within a short time.

A Dream

AFTER A DAY full of hard work, he lay down on his bed and fell immediately into a deep sleep. In his dream he saw a man of astounding beauty walking slowly and peacefully on the slope of a hill. The man moved easily and effortlessly through the barriers of religion, sect, and race that are found among humans, finally gathering all of them up and throwing them into a bottomless pit. He then moved toward the top of the hill and raised his face to the sky, saying in a voice deeper than the universe, "O God ... don't let the principles with which I was raised become a thick barrier that hides from me the truth."

War

AFTER MUCH HESITATION, the Aliens decided to visit Earth. In response to the constant messages that the Earthlings had been sending them for years, and to fulfill a longstanding desire, they laid out a program for a long and detailed study of human nature and behavior, as well as of the planet in all its aspects. Their highly advanced spacecraft took off from their planet, which was located in the farthest reaches of the universe. In record time they reached the edge of our solar system and began to monitor the Earth with their scientific instruments in most precise detail in order to send the data back to their planet. The first things their cameras detected were nuclear explosions and millions of refugees pouring out in all directions and severed human limbs piled up everywhere. Everything they photographed was killing, destruction, desolation, tongues of fire. The leader of the space fleet sent a short message to his planet saying, "We are unable to land on Earth because it is utterly consumed by a crushing civil war."

Vision

BECAUSE HIS EYES had microscopic powers it was necessary for him to pass through towering mountains and rugged declivities in the flatlands of his life.

And thus he arrived at his goal very late.

Emptying Out Sorrows

I EMPTIED OUT my sorrows into a glass and it melted ... into a wooden cup and it caught fire ... into the furnace of a man blinded by hatred and he died that instant ... into the mouth of an insane volcano and the crater was blown into the highest heavens ... into the depths of an enlightened revolution and the hearts of the people from every class of society took flame.

I returned my sorrows to my own heart ... and a smile appeared on my face.

The Strongest

FROM AMONG THE bushes, a lioness noticed a large gazelle grazing on the wide plain. She froze in place watching him, her eyes overflowing with predator instinct and a ferocious hunger that rose up from her depths. Then she began to move toward him with great care, her head lowered. Every now and again, fear jabbed at the gazelle, and he would suddenly lift his head, his weakness laid bare before the fangs of the unknown. He didn't notice the lioness until she had come within a few meters of him. Then a lightning bolt of terror lifted him into the air and sent him running like the wind. The lioness took off with utmost speed after his fresh warm meat, saliva pouring from the corners of her mouth. The gazelle moved in long, graceful leaps, changing his direction suddenly, yielding to panic and death's ringing. The survival instinct was the common denominator of beast and victim.

The image of her hungry cubs pulsed in the mind of the lioness and increased her persistence and determination to capture the rich meal that was now leaping wildly in front of her. She felt additional strength flow through her limbs and took off with great speed, wrapping her movements around her victim's provocative maneuvers until she finally caught him in a whirlwind of dust. She sank her fangs into the neck of the gazelle and her claws into his body, which flapped and flailed in every direction. The instinct for survival reached its climax in killer and victim alike. The lioness clamped down with her jaws on the tender neck with all the strength she could muster, waiting for the final silencing of the pulse.

Her cubs, who had been watching from afar, ran to her, rejoicing in the great victory. They circled around the rich and greasy meal, inhaling its appetizing odor. The hungry family began to tear apart the gazelle and devour his flesh. But then something unexpected happened. A huge male lion appeared from between the trees, saw the feast, and rushed toward them roaring. As soon as the lioness noticed him coming, she stood up preparing to defend her cubs and her spoils. The roaring of the two beasts mixed and the creatures of the forest trembled in fear. But the lioness felt her weakness before this huge, enraged male. She began to retreat, fearing that her little ones would be harmed, leaving behind the spoils upon which the lion now pounced. He dragged the gazelle easily away in his massive jaws to devour among the trees far from prying eyes.

The lioness watched him eat her torn prey, unable to do anything. The cubs looked at the scene in horror, having drawn themselves tighter against their mother. One of them turned to her and asked in a weak voice, "Mother, aren't you strong?" She answered him brokenly, "I'm very strong, my little one ... but there is someone stronger than me."

Ants

WHEN I CRUSHED a large number of ants by accident with my feet, I realized that weakness is punishment without wrongdoing.

The Door

EVERY DAY JUST before sleeping, he would make sure to go through the procedure of locking the door of the house. But after long years he discovered that he had been forgetting to do the same thing for the door of his soul so as to prevent dangerous and destructive thoughts from entering.

The God of Virtues

AFTER YEARS OF hesitation, Satan decided to make his own Facebook page and also to start a website in order to promote his principles. The idea seemed completely strange and crazy to the members of his tribe. But he tried with great enthusiasm to convince them of the plan's advantages, assuring them of its long-term success. As soon as the website and the Facebook page were online, Satan began to send out friend requests accompanied by flashy pronouncements about goodness and loving-kindness, tolerance and the brotherhood of humankind, the rejection of hatred, the embrace of human rights, and the need to fight oppression. This promotional campaign had great success among the people. Satan's happiness was indescribable. To the surprise of his tribe, his friends were counted in the thousands, and, shortly thereafter, in the millions. His site became the most famous in the whole social media world. The globe overflowed with demonstrations of support, loyalty, and admiration for Satan, waving banners soaked in the perfume of love for this champion of goodness, justice, tolerance, and equality. Humanity was fully convinced that, by the hand of Satan, the building of heaven had begun on earth.

As for the Angels of God, destructive doubt about their nature started to tear at them savagely. Little by little, fangs grew in their mouths and claws on their hands. Terrifying features formed on their faces. Embryos of evil began to pulse madly in their depths, longing to be born for humanity's destruction.

The Search

AFTER LONG HOURS lost in the forest while hiking, I finally found my way to a hut on a riverbank inhabited by a father and mother, and their daughter in her early twenties. They welcomed me in with warm affection and asked me to stay with them that night. The next morning, feeling deep gratitude toward them, I said good-bye and set off on the return journey to my house in the city. After that I returned from time to time to visit their hut whenever the opportunity permitted. A few months later, their daughter became my wife.

From this I came to understand that getting lost is a kind of unconscious search.

The Temple

AT LAST HE decided to carry out the idea that had been boiling deep inside him for many years. He withdrew all his savings from the bank and borrowed money from his family and his friends. He was full of confidence that he would quickly be able to reimburse them after putting his novel project into place.

He began building with great enthusiasm, his faith in the truth of his idea growing more firm with every stone he added to the building's foundation.

When he told his family about his project for the first time, they were greatly shocked and angered. They asked him to renounce it immediately. But he absolutely refused, trying without success to convince them of the truth of his idea. They kicked him out of the house. He felt terribly sad, but this didn't prevent him from continuing to work on his project night and day with unbending will.

News of what he was doing reached his friends and acquaintances. Their shock was so profound that they stopped talking to him. Rumors of the purpose behind his tireless building spread like wildfire. People felt hatred for him and began to throw garbage bags and stones and excrement at him. He cried bitterly, but none of this prevented him from moving forward with his project to the end.

Before a year had passed, the building was complete. He began to fill it with furniture and all the required accessories for worship. Then he started to practice rituals with utter reverence, tears streaming from his eyes.

Some of his enemies began to watch him surreptitiously from the door of the building. They looked at him in astonishment, pondering deeply his prayers. After a little while, they began to enter the building and observe him from close by. He would welcome them with absolute kindness and hospitality and offer them delicious food and drink.

Little by little the number of visitors increased, and this filled his heart with perfect happiness. He always welcomed them with open arms and a wide smile. They began asking him about his new religion ... and its rituals. He answered their questions and their inquiries with kindness and affection. The number of visitors to his temple continued to increase as news of his high principles spread. So, too, the number of believers and pilgrims, and people who came to pray also increased beyond all expectations. Because of this, he undertook to build a number of new temples both within the country and abroad. He started giving lectures and religious teachings that became wildly popular.

Within a short time, the worship of money spread through the whole world and became the official religion of every country on earth. And so ... for the first time in history a new religion emerged to unite all of humanity under its banner.

The Star Messenger

A VERY COLD night. The time is close to one in the morning. The sun goes about his work in another part of the world. The sky is clear. The stars shimmer in nervous rhythms. A killing frost lies heavy on the city—and on the body of a child who has no family, in torn clothes, six years old. It seems like he has just now emerged from the womb of tragedy that is fertile in every time and place. The cold mocks him, laughing cruelly inside his tender body. He shivers. Hunger and fear form with the cold a deadly triangle. The tatters of his clothes entwine with the tatters of his life. The streets are nearly deserted. He walks like a demagnetized compass. When hunger bites at his small body, he starts looking through bags of garbage for something to eat. Catching a crust of blackened bread in his hand, he eats it greedily. Tears flow down his cheeks without him feeling it. The cats watch their small competitor with care. And his deadly triangle watches him with utter contempt.

He sits on the ground and begins to blow on his blackened hands. He looks at the sky and sees the stars shimmering anxiously. With amazement, he says to himself, "The stars too are suffering from hunger and cold and fear ... I wish I could climb up to them to keep them company in their sadness and forget my own. How many of them there are. And how many wretched people in this world!"

A hot tear runs down his cheek ... the cold freezes it.

After a little while, as he contemplates the sky, he sees a comet fall to earth, landing far away. "The stars have sent a messenger to carry me to them," he says in a voice rising up on wings of happiness. "They definitely heard me ... but the star messenger doesn't know exactly where I am. I'll go look for him right now."

The little one stands up, struggling to overcome the deadly triangle. He sets out with quick short strides, searching for the star messenger. He walks here and there through streets and alleys. His face overflows with innocence and childlike wonder. After about an hour, despair creeps into his small heart. "Where are you, star messenger? Where are you?"

The weight of tiredness throws him to the ground. Tears flow from his eyes. With his tiny lips, he repeats the words "Oh my god" in a soft voice.

In the early morning, while a garbage man is picking up bags of garbage, he notices a small body crumpled in a corner. He comes closer and sees it is the body of a child who has surrendered to a deadly triangle.

Purity

BECAUSE HE WAS a lake of great purity, the others were able to catch his fish easily.

An Unusual Gathering

THE GROUP SAT at a rectangular table. The child sat facing the moment. The adolescent faced the minute. The young man faced the hour. The man faced the day. The middle-aged man faced the month. The old man faced the year.

"I'm tired of this. I want to get up!" the child said to the moment with agitation.

"So am I!" said the moment excitedly, "I'm leaving."

The two of them leaped up from their chairs joyfully.

"I'm getting bored here," the adolescent said to the minute. "Life is beautiful and I want to enjoy it to the last drop."

The minute agreed with him and the two of them jumped up laughing from their chairs.

"Life is a captivating woman," the young man said to the hour happily. "I won't let her pass me by."

When the hour had passed, the two of them took off.

"Life is work and struggle," the man said to the day, "there must be time to rest."

After the day had finished its twenty-fourth hour, the two of them got up and left.

"Life is tedious and tiresome," the middle-aged man said to the month. "Let's sit a while before we go."

In a month's time the two of them left.

The old man said to the year in despair, "Life has worn me down and destroyed me. We've almost ceased to exist."

The year answered him with scorn, "How stupid you are."

He wrapped the old man in a white sheet and went with him quietly through a halo of fog to a land of magical purity.

Suspect Seeds

HIS PARENTS RAISED him from his tender age in a paradise of luxury and elegance. All his requests were granted, even silly ones. The gardens of his virgin soul were sown with suspect seeds. By the time he grew up, his sense of responsibility had long ago died. He went out into the hell of reality with fancy clothes and a tattered essence. By the time he reached middle age, the black heat of the flames had burned his clothes. He spent the rest of his life in tatters inside and out.

Mutiny

THE CLOCKS ALL over the world decided to stand unified before the tyranny and absolute hegemony of time. Each clock began to move her hands as she pleased and wherever she wanted. They shouted with one voice, "Long live freedom! Down with tyranny and oppression!" They toasted their freedom and independence. After a while, however, people all over the world took off their wristwatches and pulled their clocks down from their walls and threw them all in the garbage, forming the largest clock graveyard in the world. A new generation of clocks was produced which contained a device to prevent them moving their hands as they pleased. The clocks cried bitter tears for the return of tyranny.

The Garlic and the Flower

THE OWNER OF the house put the bag of garlic he had brought from the market on the table and went into the bedroom to change his clothes. The garlic looked with disgust at a flower that was on the same table, saying, "Couldn't that fool have put me anywhere else except near this stinking thing?"

O Nothing

THE NUMBER SEVEN looked at zero standing to his left and said to him, "O Nothing! O Nobody, you are like a beggar or a bum among the humans. Nothing good or profitable can come from you!" But zero went along calmly until he came to the right side of seven. Seven was struck with surprise and looked at zero with great respect.

"Will you remain as my guest forever?" seven asked in a voice flooded with flattery. "And what would be nicer than if you invited the greatest possible number of your friends among the zeros to join you!"

Lightning and Thunder

LIGHTNING SAID TO Thunder haughtily, "I am faster than your sound and my impact is greater." She immediately launched herself in the direction of a tree in a forest and split it down the middle. Her light illuminated the forest. But only an instant later the sound of the thunder exploded and the rain fell in torrents extinguishing the fire.

Leaning on a Bone

LEANING ON A cane, the father returned home after a month spent traveling, looking for food in the wake of a famine that had totally destroyed the country. The famine had eaten what remained of his flesh and his hope. Seeing his father coming from afar, the man's four-year-old son cried out to his mother saying, "Dad's coming, leaning on one of his bones!"

The Price of Perfume

SAMER, A STUDENT in second grade, left school happy, having gotten a perfect score in math. He sped up his pace so that he could get home and tell his parents the good news.

At the corner of the street, an old man in his sixties appeared before him. His features seemed like those of an angel. His beard was long and white. When Samer was beside him, the old man leaned in close and said in a voice laden with warmth, "Do you want to perfume your hand, little one?"

Samer hesitated … His mother had told him not to talk to strangers … but never mind … the old man seemed good like his grandfather.

"Sure, grandpa," he answered innocently.

The old man took out a vial of perfume from his pocket and smeared some on the little one's hand. The boy inhaled deeply and flew high through the enchanted air. But after a moment, he fell under the burden of words smeared with muddy threats, "Give me the price of the perfume!"

Samer looked in the face of the old man and saw that the face of the grandfather had burned away to be replaced by the face of a howling wolf. He took a few steps back. Swarms of locusts invaded his virgin forests and devoured them in moments. The voice of the wolf shook him again: "Give me the price of the perfume, you little bastard!"

Through the blur of terror, Samer glimpsed its fangs. He

felt as if the whole world had changed into fangs and rabid panting. The shreds of his serenity curled into a ball inside the pupils of the monster. He didn't know how to pull his hand away from its claws. He didn't come to his senses until he was running like a rabbit from a hunter, while the threatening question beat the ground behind him with its paws: "Are you trying to rob me, you little dog?!"

The perfect score in math burned up ... the locusts settled in his soul that had been a beautiful forest ... He ran toward the house through the tunnel darkened by the howls of the wolves.

No Breathing

JUST BEFORE SLEEPING, the man pointed to the wreath of flowers on the bedside table and said to his wife, "Put the flowers on the veranda, dear, so they don't consume the air in the room." At that exact moment, the flowers were saying to each other worriedly, "If only they would sleep outside so they wouldn't breathe the air and deprive us of it."

The Big Truck

FROM MY OFFICE window I saw people running in terror as they pointed at a big tanker truck parked next to the sidewalk. It looked like Judgment Day. Some old people who were running fell to the ground and no one thought to extend a hand to them ... Shouts and screams and utterances—

"Help!" "Save us!" "We are all going to die!"—stained the horizon with their poison and their filth. Only a few minutes later the street emptied itself entirely of pedestrians.

The sight killed my desire to go down to find out what was happening. Instead I immediately picked up my binoculars and looked through them at the truck. The writing on the tank said NATION UNDER PRESSURE. FLAMMABLE!

The Blazing Planet

SO THAT HER weak points would not be known, the Earth kept her volcanoes from erupting. But she soon became a blazing planet, and finally exploded.

Her fragments flew across the universe and, millions of years later, became part of a new planet that lived far longer than the Earth because she never tried to stop her volcanoes from erupting.

A Moment of Dignity

I HAPPENED TO notice a moment of dignity flying across the sky. I promptly took an arrow and shot it down. No sooner had it hit the ground than a thousand hands rushed to grab it. I turned away brokenhearted from the torn limbs of a moment of dignity.

Meeting

THE ROCKS CALLED for an urgent meeting, but nothing came out of it except a terrible din.

Partial Paralysis

IT IS SAID that in the future the world reached an unprecedented level of development but partial paralysis disabled it, and prevented it from catching up with the progress on other planets.

Rectangular Table

LONG AGO THE leaders of the world decided to exchange the rectangular table at which they met for a round one. In this way no one would appear to have precedence. But since the beginning of life on this round globe, the disparity between nations has only become wider and deeper!

A Handkerchief of Freedom

THE DICTATOR SNEEZED. He pulled Freedom from his pants pocket and blew his nose. Then he threw her away in the wastebasket.

Struggle of Opposites

NATURE SAID, "THE world is based on the struggle of opposites."

The Tyrant added, "Under my leadership!"

Tears Without a Flame

THE CANDLE WAS astounded to see the widow weep for her recently deceased husband. "How is it," she asked herself, "that her tears are pouring down but she has no flame on her head?"

Soul Ash

IN A CAFÉ looking out over the shore of a sea of pedestrians swelling with heads and bodies of different shapes and sizes, he looked at the ash of his cigarette in the ashtray and wondered with anguish about a way to flick the ash of his burned soul when the need arose, and how to find the appropriate ashtray for such a task.

Clouds of hot steam rose in his flushed skies. He turned toward the groups of pedestrians on the sidewalk next to the café, heads rising and falling like the undulation of waves far out at sea, brains swaying with life ... with the rising and the falling.

He considered their faces, seared by the fire of melancholy and the hell of privation. He considered the old people, their backs bowed by time, getting ready to release the arrows of their souls into the next world.

Suddenly the brightly colored flag of her image fluttered in his autumn skies, and spring was born. His life opened with joy, he kissed it with tenderness … with tenderness. He inhaled deeply, its perfume still burning, a flag made from the light of angels, moved by the breeze of her scent. "Where is she now?" he asked himself again and again. "She must be married with children." But he steeled himself and looked at his memories with a cold gaze before they could continue their harrowing narrative. He felt for his pillbox in his coat pocket. He looked at the deep wound of his life resembling the crater of a volcano exhausted by eruptions and extinguished despite itself.

He felt around for the ash of his soul, wondering how to extract it and scatter it beneath the iron-wheeled vehicle of life.

Question Mark

ON A VERY clear night as I lay on the roof of my house gazing at the stars, I noticed in the empty spaces between them question marks far more numerous than the stars themselves. After a few minutes I fell into a deep sleep.

The next morning I sat on the veranda drinking a cup of coffee. I looked out on the silent plains and the mountains wreathed with clouds like giants wrapped in mystery. I saw countless question marks …

After I finished my coffee, I went inside to shave. I saw myself in the mirror, the biggest question mark an eye could see … I stepped back in terror … Since that day I have had a great hatred for question marks.

Whoever Is Happy

I STOOD ON the peak of the highest hill in the city and shouted at the people, "Whoever is happy, let him follow me!"

Only a small group answered me, no more than the fingers of one hand. As for the rest, they looked at me with suspicion and turned their backs to me.

I repeated my call, this time louder than before. But the crowd was lifeless and unresponsive. I repeated it a third time in a voice close to a scream. They looked at me with hate. Some of them pelted me with tomatoes and rotten eggs.

I changed my call and shouted again, "Whoever is sad, let him follow me!"

The people's expressions changed suddenly from sadness and indignation to joy and gladness. They ran toward me with the enthusiasm of children, answering the call of sadness with great joy. But as for the small group who had answered the first call, they paid the price of their happiness when they were trampled underfoot.

Wolves and Sheep

THE PACK OF wolves moves red-eyed through the vast forest on which Antarctic weather has fallen.

They search for prey to quiet the monsters of hunger that never grow weary of roaring night and day. The wolves' hearts tremble and they set off running over the snowdrifts as if fleeing in vain from a demon of privation.

The leader of the pack reaches the peak of one of the white hills and gazes out at the blackening horizon, its icy surface decorated by the brush strokes of twilight.

He raises his head up and lets out a long, drawn-out howl that fills the hearts of weak forest creatures with terror of the unknown. They freeze in place and prick up their ears waiting for death that could surprise them at any moment.

The roaring of the monsters of hunger runs in the blood. The leader turns in a circle and runs, chasing the scent of his instincts. The pack follows him, cutting across the barren land, passing trees exhausted by their loads of snow. "Flesh … warm fresh flesh in which the pulses of a beating heart still run, where are you? Fangs and molars have long been fully ready to devour you."

Salivary glands pulsing pulsing … the pack runs panting … instinct is panting. But surprise catches them when they see three deer drinking from the waters of a large lake. They bare their fangs and let out fearsome howls.

For a few moments the deer look at them with terror, then they melt into the ground, a pile of cold bones. The wolves freeze in their places, muted by the amazing sight, then move carefully toward the bones. They begin to sniff them and vainly turn them over with their mouths and claws. The bones are entirely devoid of any trace of flesh. They leave them and run toward the unknown, cowering before the absolute tyranny of the monster of hunger.

They keep running, panting after the trace of any weak animal betrayed by his instinctive intelligence and pushed toward ruin by his misplaced steps.

A thick snow begins to fall. The powers of nature cannot easily tear the thickly gathered weave of clouds. The forest appears entirely isolated from the world outside, bowing before nature's emergency laws. Most of the creatures flee from her dominance and tyranny into hibernation. They stay in this state, waiting for the tenderness and mercy of the spring.

The dragon of starvation runs behind the wolves ... blowing hellfire from his nostrils ... whipping them with a fiery whip ... they don't leave a burrow or a mound or a hillock until they have dug it out with frenzied claws.

They no longer see before them anything but piles of hot, fresh meat. They begin to dig in the snow with their teeth, saliva pouring from the corners of their mouths. Suddenly their leader catches sight of a little herd of goats trying to climb some trees to eat twigs and branches. He sets out toward them immediately, his followers by his side. Terror freezes the movement of the goats—they melt instantly!

The wolves attack the bones, licking their chill with the hot greed of starvation ... bearing down on them excitedly with their teeth. In their minds, amazement becomes confused with the tyranny and boundless cruelty of privation. The bones crack and become small pieces spread out on the ice ... revealing hunger's deep malice toward anyone who won't answer his call.

The wolves of the pack let out a long howl in which anger and insistence mix with sadness and pain made clear in a staccato ending that falls like small pieces of hot coals spewed by worn-out volcanoes. But the leader makes a decision from which there can be no turning back: he sends his orders to the wolves and all of them turn into little sheep of the softest and most beautiful kind. They begin to wander through the forest full of hope that their ruse will succeed and their misery will end.

After a short time they arrive at a vast plain where a great herd of deer is grazing. They go quietly toward them and spread among them waiting for the right moment to return to their original form and fall upon the appetizing prey. But in less than a moment something happens that they never expected. The deer turn into vicious, hungry wolves, their eyes windows from which fly the fires of hell. They attack the little sheep and devour them savagely. The air fills with a horrible roaring. They drag off what is left of the bloody flesh to feed their young who are waiting in their dens.

The Shadow

A TERRIBLE SHADOW spread slowly over the heads of the people, hiding from them the rays of the sun. No one dared look up to see the reason, instead they bent their heads even lower than before while the huge shadow crept ever faster. Finally their days turned into the longest of nights. Life came to a stop. Daily activities stumbled. Sadness and depression spread throughout the country. But still no one dared to think even for a second to raise his head.

Rumors began to marry crazily and beget huge numbers of sons of all shapes and colors. Some said it was punishment from God for the people's level of moral decline and their heedlessness of principles and values. Others said it was a swarm of locusts such as had never been seen in all of human history and that this plague might last for many months. Scientists maintained that the lunar eclipse and the solar eclipse had become intermeshed, forming the persistent black night. Life remained in this stumbling and sluggish state. The pillars on which its civilization had risen shattered and broke, and the country fell to earth with a terrible, loud crash. This caused its neighbors great joy and delight in its misfortune. A swampy tide of myths and rumors covered the country. The people began to suffer from pains in their backs and necks.

Finally a courageous young man appeared who decided to raise his head to the sky, despite the warnings of his family and friends, so that he might know the nature of this terrible thing that had entirely destroyed his country and returned the mindset of its inhabitants—even that of the scientists—to a primitive state.

But his surprise was great when he discovered that this disaster consisted of an extremely long tongue! He set off running as fast as he could, searching for the root of the tongue so that he could know whose it was. He discovered that it belonged to the small, ugly gang leader who, with the help of his henchmen, had prepared a strategic plan for destroying and pillaging the country for hundreds of years to come.

Never Been Touched

A BOOK SITTING on the shelf with torn covers and pages filled with comments and notes in the margins said to his colleague who stood beside him, "I envy so much your freshness and your eternal youth!"

But his colleague answered him dejectedly, "I've never been touched!"

The Sword and the Snakes

THE SWORD WOULDN'T stop complaining about the difficulties of remaining upright in a corrupt environment. But the sheath answered him: "Snakes can wrap themselves around your straightness, but this only makes it easier for you to cut them up."

Handicap

WHEN I SAW the suffering of the tortoise who had accidentally turned over on her back in my neighbor's garden, I knew that protection is a form of disability.

Bleeding

AFTER YEARS OF continuous bleeding covered in question marks, I discovered that I had been leaning on the sharp corner of life.

The Greatest Mountain

THE NIGHT WAS very clear. The lights in the steep alleys of the city and in the houses of those who loved to stay up late spread out across the mountain. Some of the lamps were making conversation.

Gazing up at the stars in the sky, a lamp said to her friend, "Look at all those lamps that fill that greatest mountain. There are so many of them! Wherever you look you find them spread thickly. Why aren't we so numerous?"

Her friend answered her as she carefully examined the multitude of stars, "Probably because the residents of that greatest mountain are far more numerous than the residents of ours."

The Fingers of Dynamite

A GROUP OF world leaders at an important international conference appeared before him on the television screen. In front of the TV cameras they were warmly shaking hands and smiling wide smiles. But his mouth gaped open in surprise as he noticed that their interlaced fingers were fingers of dynamite.

Journey to Me

TERRIBLE GUSTS OF air from within beat on the door of my soul. Coming back over a great distance, through life's iron mountains, I open it with dread. A forest trembling in the jaws of a desert of pulverized dignity invades me.

Spring feelings flatter volcanoes of anger. I hesitate to enter. I turn to the iron of the mountain. The sun reflecting off it dazzles me. I put on a diving suit and without prior experience penetrate into myself.

I see a mosaic sky. An enormous crow flies out from the eye of terror.

On the corner of one of the streets, I hear the voice of a child singing. I go toward him with quick steps. It is my childhood. I am singing a special song my mother taught me just before sleep.

On a moonlit night I go through crowded streets that flood me with loneliness. The dazzling lights of passing cars strike my eyes with fear. My curiosity grows wide.

I try to see the passengers ... in vain. An icy surface catches me by surprise. I try to slide on it slowly and deliberately, but my foot slips out from under me.

In places I am grown up ... and in others I am a child.

My teacher Sahar gives me an ornate box of sweets when she comes to visit my mother on a beautiful summer evening.

"Keep up your hard work, little one," she says as she imprints a kiss on my cheek.

In the public park I'm running toward the swing. My father runs behind me. He picks me up and sits me on his shoulders.

"You tired me out, son," he says.

I set out for neighborhoods chewed up by war, without a breeze of hope. Torn limbs of peace mix with the victims' torn limbs.

But who are these victims? I ask myself.

I pass a heavily loaded garbage container. A violent desire to excavate the past assaults me. I see sadnesses arising from the soul's internal bleeding. The teacher's slap that frigid morning when I'd been late to class appears before me. An odor seeps through the diving equipment: insults upon insults. The steam burns in my eyes. Accumulated disappointments fermenting since long ago in the deep pit of the unconscious. I dive and dive. The pressure increases drastically. The quantity of oxygen in the tank is diminishing. My father slaps my mother here. Failing the exam. Electrified wires of malice everywhere. Spite ... the seizure of the family house ... loss of money. Out from under the garbage, soiled water makes its way alone in drunken lines.

I go back and forth within my four seasons, dazed with fever at the contradictions. The pressure penetrates every cell of my body. My head begins to hurt. I turn around to see the door, but I barely hear its rebuke. I turn to the disheveled directions, dazzling lights of cars driven by unknown people. Deep darkness. The shouts of boys at the end of the school day. Hatred ... love ... success ... failure. The future nursing on the lap of a strange woman. Another icy surface appears before me. I try to slide on it ... I try ... in vain. But the others who live inside me are falling and standing up again on their feet to continue sliding excitedly amidst laughter and smiles. Isn't it strange that people should pick themselves up from their stumblings inside a person who keeps falling down?

On the horizon, flowers and grasses grow around the mouths of extinct volcanoes. Another, like a severed artery, spits hell. The rivers of lava carve alleyways in the insistence of time. What spell-weaving messengers of madness!

I begin to quicken my pace. Charmed by my world, I nearly fall into a pool of quicksand. What's worse than for a man to fall into his self's sands? I turn to face the different stages of my life, feeling always for the oxygen tank ... the pressure ... the pressure! Where are you, door? ... Where are you? I am lost inside myself!

I look up. A terrifying space. An enormous universe the mind cannot believe. One glance cannot take in more than a single star. Waves of gasping rise higher … faster. I walk forward guided by the light of a hope worn out by famine. My hands tremble. From far away comes the sound of the nursing future's cries. I climb up and down, spiraling, twisting, running here and there, afraid of myself.

Finally I reach the door. I push it open with all the terror that was in me. I tear off my diving suit. I breathe in, filling my two lungs. I sit on the ground. I look around as sweat pours off me in profusion. Night has fallen. I look at the stars. Surprise catches me and I scream, "How small you are, O universe!"

Barbed Wire

SAMIR, A CHILD not yet seven years old, was completely astounded at the behavior of his father, the famous writer who sat at his desk writing in a yellow notebook, the marks of annoyance written plainly on his face. Every now and again he would tear up the pages angrily and throw them into the wastepaper basket. This gesture was repeated many times until, unable to take it any longer, he threw the notebook far away and went off to sleep, muttering unintelligibly. Samir immediately tiptoed from the living room to the office where the wastepaper basket was. He pulled from it a piece of paper and uncrumpled it. He saw lines of barbed wire and massacred words from which blood flowed like rivers. The survivors writhed about, letting forth nightmarish cries of anguish. The child stood shocked. He threw the paper to the ground and ran to his room. He hid beneath the blanket, trembling at the terrible volcano that had erupted in his face.

Since that day, he feels great compassion for words and only inscribes them on paper completely free of barbed wire.

The Boot

HE SPENT MOST of his youth living a life of luxury and enjoying the blessings and the paradises of his country. He felt as if he were living in heaven. He even refused many offers of travel and work abroad. He loved everyone and felt that everyone loved him. Finally he decided to travel around the world to study the latest developments in the field of procuring ease and comfort, with the conviction that his country was without equal.

As soon as the plane took off and veered up in a wide circle, he was caught by surprise to notice that the layout of his country from the air took the shape of an army boot. Since that day, years and years have passed and his family and his friends are still looking for him everywhere … in vain.

Man

SA'ID WALKED OUT of the public garden with a newspaper under his arm to use as protection from the sun's scorching rays.* His face was a battlefield of hundreds of contradictory

---

* *Sa'id* is a common Arabic name meaning happy.—Tr.

emotions and electrifying questions caught between the present and the future. He hung his head as if to hide the events of the crushing battle inside him.

On the sidewalk outside the garden, a homeless person passed before him with torn clothes, a terrible smell emanating from him. All of a sudden, Sa'id became a big-bellied capitalist smoking a cigar, striding haughtily, and thinking about the profits from his last deal. He couldn't see the homeless person who stretched out his hand, wishing him success and a long life.

A little later, a luxury automobile passed in front of him, driven by a high functionary. Sa'id became a shorn sheep in a polar storm that threatened to kill him.

When he arrived at one of the fanciest hotels of the city, he became an ant born without legs, about to be crushed.

A few meters from his dilapidated house, he returned to his natural state: a low-level civil servant in a government agency, but as soon as he was face-to-face with his wife and children, he became all of them.

The Whirlwind and the Stream

I ASKED THE hurricane about his goal. He answered me in fright, "If only I knew!"

As for the stream, he sparkled in gentle bliss, knowing perfectly well where he was going.

The Shining Idea

FROM THE INVISIBLE world the child who has not yet been born looks at this life with burning desire. He contemplates the children playing in the public park. Among the shouts and laughter of their families, they swing on the swing set and slide down the slide until they are covered in dust. He wishes that he could be one of those children chided by their families so that they won't hurt themselves, finally held in big warm hands pulsing with love and compassion, rocked late in the night by a gentle voice flooding him with spring, speaking to his age, no older than the flowers, reading a fairy tale for him to sleep a little later like an angel.

He observes the plains and the mountains and the forests and the seas. He speaks in a tearful voice heard only by himself, "How beautiful is life!" He turns toward his father, who has not yet dared to marry, and speaks to him. "I beg you to get married, Father. I want to come to life and enjoy it like other children. I want to play and learn in the oasis of yours and Mom's tender love. I want to grow up and work and get married and have children and raise them well. I want to live, Dad."

His father lives in a basement. He appears like sunken sorrows and answers him with sadness: "My son, life is filled with frustration and pain and tears. You should be happy that you haven't known it. Many people wish they had not been born. It's a world full of struggle and vengeance and envy and dishonorable competition. Believe me, little one, your situation now is better than ours by far."

His son answers him with ardor: "On the contrary, Father, everything is perfectly clear to me. From the thick transparent boundary that separates me from you, I see life as exciting and full of pleasure. It's a world loud with movement and activity and success—to say nothing of the loving-kindness that floods the earth with its brilliant light. The world is a blank page."

The father answers with bitterness: "What is this loving-kindness you are talking about, Son? The world bows its head beneath the blows of malice and hate and all kinds of pollution. Every day the hell of war succeeds in swallowing new lands from the garden of loving-kindness and harmony. Failure swallows the happiness of old and young alike. The snake's hiss of idleness is heard everywhere. What should I speak to you about? About the children who search for their daily meal in garbage bins until their blank pages are polluted with the blackness of squalor? They grow up armed with all the weapons of deadly resentment. Should I speak to you about a girl who takes up prostitution when not yet ten years old because of her family's poverty and disintegration? Should I speak to you about the black defeat that humiliates the many for reasons even a devil couldn't imagine?"

His son answers him, begging: "Please listen to me, Dad. I see the children that you are speaking of playing in parks and playgrounds. They laugh and shout in extreme happiness. I want to join them. The transparent boundary that separates me from your world is very thick. You are the only one, with the help of Mom, who can destroy this barrier. Search for Mom, Dad. I beg you. Search for her. With what sorrow do I look at the mothers who feed their young from their breasts? I look with sorrow and I weep. I'm hungry for tenderness and life. The world is an entirely blank page."

His father answers him with bitterness: "No. The world is a black page. It seems that you won't understand my point of view."

The father gets up from the shredded couch and gets dressed very slowly. He heads for the door of the narrow room that for long years has contained him and the mountains of his sadness. He opens it with a trembling hand and goes out into the street steered by a brain filled with thick black smoke. His son follows him, begging and imploring, tears pouring from his eyes ... in vain. He stops, wounded, in the middle of the road, looking at his father, who with a last farewell glance has refused to have him. He begins to circle the earth, a shining idea looking for a father and a mother to be his gate to cross into this world.

Horses

I RODE THE horse of hatred. He carried me into strange places, rugged and trackless, filthy and full of wild beasts and poisonous reptiles.

I rode the horse of loving-kindness. He took me to places that enchanted my mind with their wonder and their magic to the point where I felt the sap of paradise seep into me and spread through my arteries and my veins.

But when I rode the horse of objectivity, I went through places that had a little of this and a little of that.

Thread of Light

I KEPT MY head held high with pride before the locked door of life. Because of that I didn't see the thread of light creeping out beneath the door until old age had bent my back.

The Kinds of Flowers

WHEN HE WAS human he would contemplate with joy and happiness his garden filled with different kinds of the most beautiful flowers. But when he himself turned into a flower in that garden, he began to see all other kinds of flowers as surpassingly ugly.

Convoy

THE DROPS GO calmly and quietly. The steps move forward in an orderly fashion. Smiles appear on faces. The self is utterly serene. Suddenly, a shrieking horn fills the space. Security forces rush everywhere. Everyone runs in all directions. The body is on the verge of exploding from the pressure of the screams and the shrieks. The policemen shout, "Get out of the road! Get out of the road!" Drops from all levels of society run in terror, electrified with dozens of questions. After a few moments, the highway of the Aorta becomes completely empty save for the security personnel contracted on either side. The convoy of the royal drop passes at great speed, and within minutes life returns to its normal pace.

Meanwhile, a man on the street has sat down on the closest bench, panting hard and loosening the buttons of his shirt while the sweat pours from him in profusion.

After a few days the same situation repeats itself ... shouts of the policemen ... the Aortic highway completely emptied of blood ... security forces contracted on both sides ... the royal convoy with its speed so great the man loses consciousness. He is brought to Intensive Care.

A month later the story repeats itself, and he dies of a heart attack.

The Swamp and the Stream

THE SWAMP ASKED the stream with disdain, "Why are you so skinny?"

"Because I never stop working," the stream answered hurriedly.

Darkness of Man

ON A CLEAR night someone was knocking savagely at his door. The door finally broke under repeated blows. A man with a thick mustache and a hellish face entered, his shoulders covered in stars. The man slapped him and kicked him: blood flew from his nose and mouth. Then he was dragged into a small, colorless car, where the man carried on his task with the cooperation of his colleagues until he became a torn old sock. They threw him along with other torn socks into a subterranean cell like the artery of an old man who had just died from smoking. It did not take long before they moved him to a separate cell where they carried on their work with great enthusiasm until he turned into human dust. They came out brushing the dust off their uniforms and off the stars on their shoulders.

Through the tiny window of that cell, a star had looked down in terror, saying to herself, "We light up the nights of humankind, and these ones, with their stars, turn life to utter darkness."

Hospitality

HE UNDERTOOK TO enlarge his house as much as possible so that he could receive the greatest number of guests. Hundreds were able to enter and enjoy the finest pomp and splendor in the house that had become a palace, yet only steps away from him the whole of humanity lived in happiness in the vast heart of his old servant.

Hell Between Two Heavens

SHE WAS BORN to wealthy and loving parents, but after a few years her mother and father fought bitterly and separated. She began to travel between their separate mansions. Neither one of them was stingy with money or love for her, but she suffered greatly in the hell of the road from one to the other. She would have loved to reunite the two mansions, to cut off the hellish road. She cried and begged. She sought the help of friends and relatives to no avail. In the end, while making her way she fell into the tongues of flame, looking all the while at the two heavens shimmering on opposite sides.

The Pearl of the Moment

I TRIED TO return to the pearl of the moment that had brought me together with her. I found it living inside an oyster. I tried to open the oyster with a knife but when I did, the oyster shuddered. I put it back in its place and returned to my moment.

The Dark Side

THE MOON WISHED to punish humans for the many transgressions and frightful crimes they commit against each other and against nature. She decided to hide her lighted side so that they would curb their behavior and return to reason. And so the eclipse took place. But great was the surprise of the moon when she saw millions of people coming out of their houses to enjoy the view of her dark side.

Flag of Surrender

A THORN DARINGLY pierced a jasmine petal and felt proud. She didn't realize that in so doing she had become a flag of surrender.

Arrest

THE KING WAS filled with great anger at the flashes of lightning and explosions of thunder that left him sleepless on ferocious winter nights and caused him to pace back and forth in his vast room in the beautiful palace overlooking the loveliest lake of the capital. He issued an order calling for the arrest of the lightning and the thunder and ordered their detention in two adjoining cells.

The order was carried out. The king said to his wife, "I wonder what is the real reason behind the lightning's impetuousness? His energy is easily transmitted to me and makes me very nervous. This is what pushed me to throw him into prison—I was afraid that this unnatural state would have a negative effect on my decision-making and this, in turn, would cause harm to my people, whom I love and respect a lot, as you know."

His wife, who had been working on her makeup in front of the mirror for three hours, answered him with a careless shrug.

But the king also wanted to know the secret behind the mad flights of the thunder. He summoned the greatest scientist in the country and asked him about it. The scientist answered without daring to look in his eyes, "The reason, my lord, is the clouds colliding with each other."

Overflowing with happiness, the king shouted, "For this good news with which you have warmed my heart, you will receive a reward such as you never dreamed of in your life! And so, in this way, I have put an end to the wars and misunderstandings among the clouds! I have spread the principle of tolerance and acceptance of others. Loving-kindness will overflow the sky with its pure white flowers!"

He began to walk back and forth, rubbing his hands together with evident enthusiasm. A wide smile never left his face. He immediately ordered the scientist, who was struck dumb with surprise, to be given a monetary reward that would drown him and his grandchildren for years.

As for the lightning, its impetuousness and nervous energy continued for some time. But then he stopped eating the meals of meteors and starlight that were passed to him through the tiny window of the cell. He began to waste away little by little until he turned into a long, thin, broken white thread huddled in one of the corners of the cell. At the same time the awesome roars of the thunder turned into the mewing of a kitten exhausted with hunger and cold. The rain stopped falling on the country. The land became wasted and dry. Crops failed and animals perished. People began to eat each other.

The king lived happily because of his unprecedented victory in spreading the principles of tolerance and acceptance of others among the clouds.

The Name

DESPITE HIS BEST efforts, the Author's name began to slide down off the top of the book's cover where it had been printed. The Author's self-confidence had died long ago, but his name was determined to hang on to the spot where it belonged with all its might. It dug its nails into the smooth cover as the sweat poured off, but its body, which had become unbelievably heavy, pulled it stubbornly down. Every so often it glanced fearfully into the abyss below it, where terrifying creatures paced, snapping their jaws hungrily. Its tears mixed with its sweat. Its body grew emaciated and its nails broke off. Clinging to the bottom edge of the cover, it peered up with diminishing eyesight at the high peak where it had once sat. A moment later it dropped into the pit and was crushed by thousands of feet walking this way and that in a frenzied haste. As for the book, years later it was hailed as an anonymous literary masterpiece.

The Fingernail

THE FINGERNAIL CLIPPING looked up at the crescent moon with sadness.

"When will our Lord know our sufferings?" she asked herself. "When will he come down from his ivory tower and hear our complaints? How great is the distance between us and him! How must the world look from his position! No doubt it's beautiful ... terrifyingly beautiful!"

The Dairy Woman

AS THE YOUNG farmer was milking his cow at the farm, his wife came to him, carrying their baby. She sat on a rock near him and took out her breast and began to nurse the child. When the cow saw her doing this, she said to herself with annoyance, "Why doesn't this intruder leave me alone and be content to milk his female!? What is this daily annoyance? I want my children to get their fill of my milk. I never saw a man milk his female even once. Is it simply because we're cows? What kind of slavery is this!"

Fate

IN A CROWD of ants, two were conversing at some distance from the others. One asked the other, "What is the truth about fate in your view?"

Pursing her lips, her friend thought for a little and said, "I think it is an enormous power, so much greater than we are that we cannot escape. What's more, its greatness is such that it can bring you down or lift you up without even being aware you exist. Sometimes—"

Just then the enormous foot of a child playing with a ball took them by surprise, crushing a large number of ants. The two of them miraculously escaped the massacre. The child continued playing without feeling a thing. The two friends ran away as fast as possible, trembling in terror. When they reached a safe place and their rapid breathing had subsided, the second ant told her friend, "That is fate, my dear, that is fate."

Why Don't Women Lay Eggs?

FROM THE CHICKEN coop two chickens heard their mistress screaming as she gave birth to her child.

"Imagine," one said to the other, "the human female bears her young without a shell to cover them. No doubt this is the reason behind her screaming and wailing like a madwoman: she suffers a terrible wound and blood pours from her in profusion. I saw this once with my own eyes. And this is also the reason behind the cries of her newborn young. They too suffer a lot as a result of this unnatural delivery, and some of them even die soon afterward—like what happened to my mistress last year. What could be easier or safer than the way we chickens give birth!"

"Alas for human females," replied her friend.

Man and the Law of Nature

MAN ARRESTED THE Law of Nature and put her in a diamond cage. He caressed her with his genius and mocked her with the products of his reason. To celebrate the occasion, he drank dozens of glasses of wine and fell down drunk, pulses of happiness settling in his heart. The Law of Nature snuck her hand over to one of the glasses and emptied it into her stomach down to the last trace of its perfume so that she might forget her prison. She grabbed a second and a third and a fourth. She lost her balance and weaved from side to side. She laughed and cried and vomited and beat her head against the diamond bars. She fell down, her forehead covered in blood. She mustered the remnants of her eroded powers and finished off the rest of the wine. She fell into the lap of death, and death held her close, hugging her and man together.

Who Deserves a Muzzle?

THE OWNER OF the house, wanting to sleep soundly, put a muzzle on the dog. But no sooner had he done so than a bloody fight broke out between him and his sharp-tempered wife over something or other. Their shouts shook the corners of the house and they disturbed the neighbors with their screaming. The dog looked at them, astonished, saying to himself, "Who deserves this muzzle ... us or them? Who deserves these collars that they wrap around our necks as if they would strangle us? We endure their cruelty and their arrogance and give them abundantly of our fidelity, more than they ever give each other. When we want to give vent to our repressed feelings in our beautiful barking tongue—just as they do in their language despite its inherent inanity—they muzzle our mouths for no purpose other than to exercise their madness." Sighing in agony, he continued, "Our grandfathers spoke the truth when they said, 'A muzzle for men, eloquence for dogs!!'"

Zebra Running on Two Legs

WHILE A HERD of zebras grazed on the plain, one of them noticed a man running in flight from a nearby prison wearing the special uniform of prisoners so like the colors of those animals.

"Look ... look at that zebra running on two legs!" he said to his friends with surprise. Everyone stared in wonder.

"His form is truly strange," said another. "I wonder where he's coming from?" The answer came from a friend: "I've heard of a gathering place near here where this kind of zebra congregates."

Here the elder zebra, who was respected by all and considered their sage, sighed and said in a deep voice, "This is one of the wonders of this world, dear ones."

As the fleeing prisoner disappeared from sight, the zebras' eyes remained fixed on their elder in surprise.

Who Leads Whom

THE DONKEY HAD not walked more than a few meters carrying his master, the traveling salesman, on his back, when he suddenly stopped and would not move. The salesman spurred him with his two feet, but in vain. He got down and pulled him by the bridle with all his strength, without result. He began cursing him with every insult that came to mind. The donkey brayed in protest saying, "I think it's your turn to carry me! You know that I won't move from here until you carry me on your back—I have carried you these long years. It's very strange, sir: don't we, the community of donkeys, deserve to revolt even once against the degradation and shame that we are exposed to throughout our lives? It's not possible to reach an understanding with you on the matter of our rights and how to protect them when you speak a strange language and your voices are the pinnacle of ugliness! There is no means other than revolt. If only you could understand this, you who think you belong to a species that is preternaturally smart!"

The Harshness of the Sun

ON THE OTHER side of the earth, the moon looked at the sun with doubt, asking him, "Why do you prevent people from looking at you in the midday hours? I let them stare at me and enjoy my beauty from my first appearance as a crescent until I become a full moon, filling the universe with its wonder and inspiring in poets and artists the most beautiful poems and melodies."

The sun looked at her and said in a voice full of power and confidence, "The midday, my dear, is for work and making a living. I allow them to enjoy my beauty at dawn and in the evening. How many poets have sung of my rising and my setting? How many lovers have exchanged passionate kisses in those hours?"

When the moon heard his answer, she knit her brows and didn't utter a word.

Who's the Best?

FOR A LONG time the ceiling of one of the rooms of the poor farmer's house had been acting haughtily toward the floor. He never stopped repeating night and day, "I am higher than you. I am the symbol of lofty ambition. As for you, feet trample you and you are covered in dirt."

Exasperated, the floor would only look at him with hatred and wouldn't answer.

One day the farmer discovered a jar of gold in the floor. The floor shook with laughter, saying mockingly to the ceiling, "They hide treasure in me and not in you."

Then the ceiling wished the ground would open and swallow him up.

They Don't Know How to Bark

IN THE YARD, two dogs, one black and one white, looked at their master cutting the grass. The black one said to his friend, "Don't you see how pitiful it is that those humans suffer from a weak sense of smell? ... For us it's enough to smell even the trace of one of them in order to be able to follow him however far. To say nothing of the fact that we can distinguish smells from a distance of hundreds of meters. We sense danger immediately, no matter how hidden. As for them, they can't smell unless you stick something right under their nose."

The white dog shook her head in scorn, saying, "As if it weren't enough that they are so stupid, they don't even know how to bark!"

Greatest Creatures

THE MOTHER ANT urged her son to hurry up and carry what remained of the winter reserves.

"I'm tired, Mom," the son whined.

"What are you talking about, Son?" answered the Mother. "The thing which most distinguishes us—the community of ants—from the rest of the creatures is our colossal energy and struggle. This is precisely what makes us the greatest creatures on earth."

Her son answered her with a little doubt, "But I've heard some of my friends saying that humans are the greatest creatures and the strongest in their capacity for struggle."

The mother shook her head mockingly, saying, "Those creatures that you think are the greatest and the strongest in their capacity for struggle have wasted tens and hundreds of years since the beginning of their existence until now in wars that resulted in nothing but the destruction of the beautiful heritage that they had built and the death of millions of them. No doubt they had a lot of geniuses who brought to their nations incalculable benefits, and were it not for this destruction they would be far better off than the state they are in now. This species, son, takes one step forward and many steps back. It is not an example for us to follow in any way. Now come on! Let's get back to work."

Arrogance

MY WEALTHY BROTHER lent me a sum of money wrapped in a thick shell of arrogance. I tried to break it with a stone ... but in vain. I hit it against the wall ... I used a hammer and an anvil ... without result. I returned it to my brother, who tried to solve the problem using every method. But the shell maintained the hardness of arrogance. He put it back in his pocket ... and the arrogance melted.

Get On Before Me?

WHILE IN THE train station, I noticed people from the Third World boarding trains heading toward the past. Meanwhile, people from the First World were boarding trains bound for the future. After a short while, two men from the Third World caught my eye. They were trying to board a train to the future. Each of them was beseeching the other in God's name to get on board before him.

While this was happening, the train left the station, moving very fast. The two men remained frozen in their places, stupefied with amazement. But then they quickly went off toward the train of the past, pushing and shoving each other violently.

A Bomb in the Traditions

I PLANTED A nuclear bomb in the folds of worn-out traditions. After the explosion they remained as they had been, only more worn-out than ever.

Embrace

IN A PLEASANT garden, the trees embrace over two quarreling brothers.

Lost Opportunities

I LEFT BEHIND me a great number of lost opportunities. I piled them up in one of the corners of my memory and did everything I could to forget them. But their bodies began to decompose and filled my life with their hateful smell.

The Faithful Friend

THE SHIP WAS overjoyed when she glimpsed the beam from the lighthouse through the sea's agitation. She said happily to herself, "Here is a friend who is never unfaithful."

At the same time, the lighthouse was saying to herself with determination, "I will not betray her trust as long as I live."

From the Depths of the Future

THE SECOND WORLD WAR said proudly to her colleague, the First, "Inside me are millions of victims!" The First World War answered her irritably, "I didn't fall short in my duties either." But just then a huge sound invaded them from the future, stating, "*I* will devour everyone!"

Peace Agreement

STRONG AND WEAK signed a peace agreement. Weak had the document framed in a gold frame and hung it in the front room of his house. He called a press conference to publicize the event with photographs and articles. He considered it a rebirth for himself. Strong, on the other hand, used his copy to make a diaper for his baby.

Flowers of Different Classes

A FLOWER PLANTED on the edge of the veranda looked spitefully at another flower inside the house. She asked her companion, "Why should that worthless plant be welcomed inside while we are left out under the burning sun to die of thirst?"

"She must have known an important flower!" her friend replied.

The Flag and the Fire

A FLAG HANGING slack from his flagpole observed with pain that the flames of a fire a few meters away were dancing happily. "What sort of breeze is it that makes you flutter like that?" he asked. The fire laughed surreptitiously but didn't say a word.

Journey

MY IMAGINATION TOOK me on a journey to wonderful lands of great civilization. Unfortunately, he was so taken with the way of life there that he decided to settle down. He sent me back alone to live out my life without him.

Insult

A MAN OF principles was forced to swallow an insult. He choked and died. As for the bootlicker, he chased after the insult with all his might, fearing that he would die of hunger.

Human Malice

BOASTING TO THE nuclear bomb, the grenade said, "You can't even imagine all the malice I have inside!"

"What is your malice compared to mine?!" the bomb replied.

But human malice heard them and admonished them, saying, "I made you both, you fools!"

Trying to Pass

ONE OF THE minutes tried to pass her companion in front of her, but the hand of time slapped her so hard she was thrown back a couple of minutes. She was just starting to recover when she was slapped again, back into her place in time.

Bone Separation

THE PRISON GUARD brought in an enormous pile of bones and said to the prisoner haughtily, "If you can separate the animal bones from the human ones we will set you free immediately." He went away with a sadistic laugh. The prisoner spent years trying in vain to separate out the bones. Eventually he fell dead over the pile, and his own bones, little by little, were lost among the others.

When the Sparrow Was Imprisoned

THE MOMENT THEY locked up the Sparrow, Freedom felt his pulse weaken and lose strength. Tears ran down his cheeks and carried away with them all his happiness. The Cage, however, at the very same moment, was buoyed up by an overwhelming feeling of joy: he had found meaning in his life at last.

Stones

THE THIRD-WORLD COUNTRIES tumbled down toward the lake of life, filling the air with the noise of slogans and abuse. But soon they settled at the bottom, and quiet prevailed again.

The Light and the Pupil

THE UNRESTRAINED LIGHT said resentfully to the eye's pupil, "You are such a coward!"

The pupil quietly replied, "I have enough room for fools."

A Bag of Poverty

AFTER SEVERAL YEARS of desperate attempts, the people had finally been able to gather poverty from all over the world and compact it in one huge bag, holding their noses all the while because of the awful stink. They threw it into a bottomless garbage container. A few moments later, the container spit the bag out with all its strength so that it flew high in the air. The bag split apart, scattering sticky chunks all across the world. This time poverty filled not only the earth but also the sky with its wretched smell!

Giant Flute

AS THE SHEPHERD played on his little reed flute, his instrument stared sorrowfully at the barrel of a nearby cannon, thinking, "I wish I were as big as that flute! I bet his melodies reach far across the world."

And in a little while the giant flute began to play his tune.

Closed Society

I HAVE LIVED in a closed society all my life. Once, it started to open up, but the smell was so bad that it closed right back in on itself again.

A Weak Point

THE ACTIVE VOLCANO boasted to a passing cloud, "My anger is such that no one can stand in my way—I can wipe all towns and cities from the map!" Irritated, the cloud ordered him to be silent: "You are nothing but a weak point in the body of the earth, like a pimple on a human body!" The volcano kept silent. The cloud kept moving.

Do Not Forget the Poor

EVEN BEFORE I arrived at the corner, a few meters from my friend's house, I smelled a very sad smell. I felt a pain in my stomach, and I found it very strange. When I reached the corner, the sad smell became unbearable. My tears began to fall profusely, leaving me confused. Then I saw a woman in the autumn of her life. Her clothes were torn, like her life. She was covered with the tears of Humanity. I went toward her, shaking from the pain, which increased as I drew nearer. When I was beside her, she looked up at me and said with tears in her voice, "Don't forget the poor!"

My soul fell into scattered pieces. Humanity looked me right in my eyes, and the contraction of her pupils squeezed my heart. I took a handful of coins from my pocket and gave them to the old woman. Humanity grasped my hand in support. As she took the money, she looked at me with two eyes that gazed into the deepest depths of tragedy. And as soon as the money was in her hand, the sad smell disappeared and the pain in my stomach dissolved. My tears stopped. Humanity patted me on the shoulder and took from the pocket of her white garment a quantity of happiness that would last me for thousands of days, and she planted it in my future. I turned to my friend's door, but just as I was ringing the doorbell, the old woman let out a volcanic scream that burned the embryo of my happiness, and fell down dead.

Employee's Paycheck

AS SOON AS the Paycheck, who had been born handicapped, reached the eighth step of the month's stairway, he tripped and fell down and died.

The Stake

THE GREAT WRITER was forced to sit on his own pen as punishment for his sharp tongue. The ink shot up into him until his blood turned blue. He became one of the elite ... and slowly came to his senses.

The Cage

THE BIRD LOOKS sadly through the bars of the cage at the vast space perfumed with the scent of freedom. He dreams of the treasure of which he was long ago deprived. He inhales deeply its heavenly smell and sorrow sears his heart. He considers his brothers and all his fellow birds who enjoy the fruits of that treasure and says to himself with anguish, "How much I wish I could be with them, spreading my wings wide, surrendering to the waves of air and the refreshing gusts, enjoying freedom's boundless wealth!"

He looks at the bars of the cage, his gaze heavy with the fetters of captivity. He feels as if they were wrapped around his heart with utmost cruelty. His throat fills with a hymn of wounded pride.

But the bright white specter of freedom, opening his arms, appears suddenly one day when the bird's owner forgets to lock the cage after putting food inside. The innumerable wings of the bird's soul start to tremble before the two wings of his body do. He surrenders to the azure waves, flying through their colorful current, rising and falling, amazed at these wonders which he had all but forgotten.

He pursues his flight enthusiastically, searching for his family and friends, of whom slavery's bars had deprived him. He swoops through freedom's atmosphere, enchanted by her wonderful melodies, looking carefully in all directions. The captivating perfume of his pride, which has now completely recovered, mixes with the remains of the scents of his loved ones scattered in the air.

Pearls of happiness lie interspersed among hot coals of questions: "Where are you, my beloved ones? In what spaces are you flying? My longing for you is the rope of light that binds me to you and that will guide me toward you no matter how much time should pass!"

After a few days, as he flew near a high mountain, the bird recognized one of his brothers. He set out toward him, panting from gusts of happiness while freedom gazed at the coming together of the brothers' souls and the harmony of their bodies, and added to her store of laughs a new enchanted one.

The two of them, setting out with their friends for journeys brimming with the elixir of happiness, formed a swooping flock intoxicated by lofty spiritual feelings for which no name has been discovered.

But the bird who had been set free suddenly felt a strange body growing inside him, a body he recognized, growing heavier and colder in opposition to the warmth of his own. It was a cage made from the strongest kind of steel. The bird was shocked by the horror of this feeling. The cage grew broader and heavier forcing the wretched bird to fly dizzily up and down amidst the astonishment of his friends. Finally, when the weight of the cage had grown far too heavy for him, he fell at the edge of the forest.

He became easy prey for the first carnivorous animal that passed his way.

The Souls of Flowers

FROM HIS EARLIEST childhood, he was used to taking care of flowers with special attentiveness. He would water them several times a day and talk gently to them, speaking spiritual words overflowing with love and clarity, not forgetting to smile broadly. This would fill the flowers with blissful joy. To the astonishment of his family and friends, he kept up this habit until the last moment of his life. When he died, the souls of the flowers that had preceded him into the next world years before were the first to come and welcome him.

Respect

I HAVE SEEN humans with the eyes of mice, and mice with the eyes of intelligent humans.

I have seen donkeys refuse absolutely to have even one straw placed on their backs, and humans accept huge rocks to carry without anything being given to them in return.

I have seen a creature made entirely of ears and, even so, unable to hear a thing. And I've seen an earless creature who could hear everything.

I have seen the skull of the present wearing the beautiful mask of the past.

I have seen masters behaving like slaves, and slaves behaving like masters.

I have seen tails turn into snakes that never grow tired of biting.

And so I hold all creatures in great respect until their opposites appear.

Hooray

THE CLOCK ON the wall stared at a bucket sitting in the sink. The clock listened to the drops of water falling regularly into the bucket. She said to herself, "How is it that the time of that clock is gathered together, but mine is not? This isn't fair!"

After a while, the bucket became full to the top with water and the drops started to overflow. The clock on the wall shouted loudly, "Hooray for justice! Hooray for justice!"

Why Do They Hit Us Against One Another?

WHEN THE CONCERT ended, the hands in the audience began a loud round of applause. One hand protested, saying to the other, "Why do they violently hit us against each other? Look how they are laughing and cheering! They are such criminals!" The hand looked at the members of the orchestra, who were now bowing to the audience: "And why are they bowing?" Trying not to show its pain, the other hand replied, "They respect violence!"

The Flowery Day

THE DAYS OF the week were arguing about which one was most distinguished and so deserved the title "The Flowery Day." Their argument grew so bitter that they began to edge away from each other more and more. This made life's journey slower and slower.

The Beautiful Face

I SAT ON the top of a hill looking into the amazingly beautiful face of history. It seemed to me that his beauty surpassed even the most wonderful human form in charm and loveliness. I went down from the top of the hill and walked toward him. I was dazzled and taken by him, and I carried in my heart a bouquet of flowers that multiplied continuously. But as soon as I came near him, I noticed something terrifying in his wonderful eyes: his pupils were the openings of two giant cannons firing interchronological missiles through the ages. From his precisely drawn mouth came slanderous insults and profanities that crossed the centuries, and hatreds and grudges that didn't recognize the boundaries of time. I turned and went back to my house, cursing the splendor of a history that is eager to destroy the future.

The Hedgehog and the Snake

NEAR A RIVER in the middle of the forest, the poisonous snake was at a loss. She couldn't find the right way to bite the hedgehog who had curled up into himself as soon as he noticed her slithering in his direction. She tried hard to find a good place to bite the thorny ball, but without success. She let out a long hiss, saying to him in great annoyance, "You wicked thorny wretch!" The hedgehog answered her, smiling, "It's better to be thorny on the outside than on the inside, O snake with your beautiful skin."

Strength

I LAY ON the riverbank enjoying the gentle breezes. A few meters from me, a feather, blown violently in every direction, was cursing the storm.

The Head of Hair and the Guillotine

JUST BEFORE THEY led him to the guillotine, they cut the long hair which flowed over his shoulders. One of the hairs said to her companions, "Why do they do this when we are by nature such weak creatures? They can bend us and wrap us and move us and tie us up however they like." Another hair answered her, saying, "Despite all this weakness ... in union there is strength."

Interior Renovation

I NOTICED THAT my neighbor who lives in the apartment opposite mine was coming outside to throw out bags of garbage dozens of times every day, sweat pouring off of him. They were big bags. I was surprised at this because I knew him well, and I knew that he wasn't moving or renovating. Finally, when my surprise reached its peak, I asked him the reason. He answered me with obvious happiness, "It's my psychological garbage."

Between the Donkey and the Horse

WHEN THE WILD horse was taken captive, he felt violent anger mixed with despair. He persisted in a state of rage and revolt, and none of those who had captured him could break him. While this was happening, a wild donkey who had just been captured was brought into the stable. He was completely calm. The donkey observed the horse's rebelliousness and rash anger. Surprised, he asked him, "Why so much rebelliousness, my friend? The matter is much more simple than you imagine." The horse looked at him with disdain and replied, "The matter is simple for those who accept servility and humiliation."

Tree

WHEN ONE OF them, in a moment of anger, cut down a giant historic tree, I hoped that the direction of its fall would not be toward the present and the future.

Homeless Buildings

THE CIVIL WAR burned up all stability and spread its ashes everywhere. The people fled the city, which had been almost entirely destroyed. Because of this the city's buildings felt lonely and drew very close to each other until they were almost touching. Warmth spread between them. They looked like homeless people in torn clothes gathered around a fire on a cold night. Years later ... after the end of the war, the people of the city came back and began to rebuild, but when they did so, the buildings kept their new closeness. And because of this, human relationships became far warmer and closer than they had ever been before.

Fuel

IN THE BITTER cold of winter, he would fire up his soul as a furnace and invite countless people to warm themselves at its fire. In the intense heat of summer his soul became a wonderful air conditioner whose delicious coolness would penetrate the pores of their souls. He would look at them with happiness and his conscience was easy, even though it never crossed the minds of any one of them to invite him or anyone else to their soul's furnace in winter or to their air conditioning in summer. They were only bent on saving fuel. But he never stopped welcoming increasing numbers of people year after year because he knew that the soul's fuel has no price and can never run out.

Human Destiny

WITH A FEARFUL heart, I opened the door of human destiny. Hundreds of crows flew into my face, their caws deafening my ears. I saw the future lying on a torn couch. Near his head was a red table on which were placed long lines of medicine bottles and three extinguished candles. His body was withered and wrinkled. His chest rose and fell with tragic speed as the angel of death, full of childlike happiness, jumped up and down on him. With difficulty I tried to pierce the terror of the death vigil. At his feet was a pile of dead hopes, falling continuously from the human family tree. The ceiling was low like a person crowned with shame. The walls were narrow like the mind of man blinded by fanaticism. I put my trembling hand on the forehead of human future. I jumped back at the extreme heat. I held his gnarled hand and, looking at his protruding veins and ravaged nails, I kissed it. He looked at the ceiling with eyes lost in the desert of existence, as the rhythm of the angel of death jumping up and down on him grew faster. He opened his mouth with a Herculean struggle and spoke coded words. In vain I tried to translate them. The cawing of the crows burst my eardrums. The dead hopes fell over me. After a few trembling moments he gave up his soul, letting out a scream that destroyed the pillars of humanity.

Kicks

THE TWO INTERROGATORS had left their prisoner curled in a corner of the room, bleeding profusely and shaking in terror. Soon the corner itself administered a kick that sent him tumbling across the room. In this way the four corners went on kicking him back and forth until the roof collapsed on him and finished the job.

The Beast

IN A LUSH garden, two friends sat eating on a bench. A small multicolored bird landed on the ground in front of them. One of them said to the other, "That bird is so beautiful—it's a symbol of life's gentle-hearted beauty."

At that moment, the bird flew toward the branch of a tree

where it had noticed a caterpillar crawling. The caterpillar tried to crawl away with all its strength, screaming in terror, "The beast has come!"

The Forbidden Doll

FIVE-YEAR-OLD SAMAR SAT on the edge of the bed looking at her doll lying on the couch on the opposite side of the dark room ... her beloved doll that her father had given her for her last birthday. She didn't dare to bring her over to the bed to play with her. Her father's wife had hit her really hard with a stick yesterday when she dropped a full pitcher of water on the clean floor. Today too she'd gotten four lashes on her face from the whip of her stepmother's hand because she'd stained her clothes with candy. That's why she had been locked in her room from three in the afternoon until the next morning, with the blinds closed firmly and with only a small cheese sandwich on a glass plate for food.

Now ... night had fallen ... and all kinds of feelings crowded around her. Darkness became an oppressive force, toying with her nerves, unleashing its black silence.

The only thing that calmed her was the thin light creeping in from under the locked door of her room and the scattered sounds coming from the street. She felt around with her small hand for the sandwich on the table. When she found it, she swallowed it greedily, surprising herself at the speed with which she gulped down the last mouthful ... then she felt thirsty ... but her stepmother hadn't left her a glass of water.

"She must have been in a rush and forgotten," Samar said to herself.

She felt lonely for her father's lap and his warm chest ... she felt lonely for his smile perfumed with tenderness. But he was away on a business trip and wouldn't be back for a month. Suddenly she was again drawn by the charm of her doll whose image flooded her mind. She stretched her torso forward and whispered in a gentle voice, "How are you, my beautiful doll? I'm sorry: I forgot to give you some of my sandwich."

She burned with desire to pick up the doll that was hidden in thick blankets of darkness and hold her to her chest and play with her and talk to her forever.

With her small body, she slid off the edge of the bed and touched the ground with her feet, watching the thin thread of light slipping in from under the door of the room.

Where did she get the courage to cross all that distance and bring back her beloved doll? The essence of her life and her existence ... Her stepmother could come in at any moment and catch her in the criminal act, playing with her doll when she had ordered her to sleep right away. And Samar didn't want to make her angry. She's a good woman .... That's what Samar told herself.

She went back and jumped up on her bed and lay there with her eyes open, her imagination like a wild pony running far off in meadows of dreams.

She heard the voices of kids playing and having fun in a neighboring apartment. Sleep wouldn't come ... She wished she could be with them. She smiled, really seeing herself with them, holding hands in a circle and spinning around, playing hide-and-seek .... She played happily.

Suddenly a dog barking in the street brought her back to the injustice of her reality .... Her doll called out to her again in a voice more insistent than before. She got down from the bed, unable to resist her desire, and walked with utmost difficulty through a minefield of terror. When she was about halfway from the bed to the sofa where the doll was lying, she heard footsteps coming near the room ... Embalmed by fear, she watched a shadow erase the thread of light under the door. The darkness stayed pinned there for a few immortal seconds and then was wiped away as the footsteps of disaster continued on their way. She ran back to her bed and hid herself under the comforter, holding on to it with all her strength ... In the boiling torrent of her emotions, tears flooded from her eyes ... and after a little while she slept, dreaming of her doll.

The Dog and the Nation

YESTERDAY AS I was heading to work in the early morning, I saw two big flyers posted side by side on a fence outside the public park. One of them had a picture of a small white dog with the word LOST written above it. The other one had a strangely shaped map with the words LOST NATION written above in red. What surprised me was the huge number of people packed around the picture of the beautiful white dog, words of regret and distress crowding about them more thick than the crowd of people; while the flyer for the missing nation remained neglected, not drawing the attention of a single person.

The Veil

I THREW THE thin and brilliantly colored veil of imagination over the rocky terrain of reality. It became a beautiful sight, but the topography remained just as it had been.

Marriage

WHILE I WAS jogging in the park near my house, a small man passed in front of me. As he went by me, a terribly cold breeze rose out of him that filled my body with trembling. A short while later, an old man passed close to me who made me feel like the fire of an oven had blown through me. I jogged away, looking back at him in shocked amazement. Soon after that, a woman came near me who froze me and burned me in the same instant ...

Since that day, I am convinced that humans must be the result of a marriage between heaven and hell.

Two Cars

TWO CARS STOPPED at a stoplight, an old model and a new one next to each other. The new one looked at the old one with amazement. Her eyes had rarely seen this kind of car, which almost no longer existed.

"I pity you," she said. "You were made by a primitive hand lacking a scientific, creative touch and the power of inventiveness! Look at me ... I'm a miracle in motion."

Feeling insulted, the old car answered her, saying, "You may enjoy the benefits of advanced technology on the inside, but your body is weak and fragile and can't take even the smallest shock. My strong body has the power to withstand any shock." Going on, she added in a deep voice, "You're like a modern human: a weak body and an utterly complicated inner life full of complexes and negativities and bad tendencies. Me, I'm like a premodern human possessed of a pure and simple soul, living in the heart of nature and eating from its goodness. Humans back then were built with a strong constitution that could resist disease."

But the new car didn't even hear the last sentence. As soon as she saw that the light had turned green, she started off as fast as possible, leaving behind her old colleague, who was trying hard to keep up with the rest of the new model cars.

The Broken Diamond

A DIAMOND RAN into a friend of his in the street and found him shattered into small pieces. With a mixture of surprise and disapproval, he asked, "What did this to you? We are the diamond race. Nothing can break us."

His friend answered sadly, "I am a great man born in the wrong time and place."

Honeyed Words

STARTING FROM HIS wide smile, a flood of honeyed words poured out of him day and night. And so he became an easy trap for insects and particles of dust.

Evil Twins

A PREGNANT WOMAN wished to have a sonogram to know the gender of the fetus. Two twin children appeared to her on the screen. The features of one were angelic, but the other's were satanic. The woman was struck with terror. An episode of deep depression invaded her that lasted the whole length of her pregnancy. Her appetite grew weak. She became nervous and began to smoke voraciously … When they were born, both children had satanic features.

The Sorrows of the Empty Pen

JUST AS THE great poet arrived at the middle of the poem that he had begun early that morning, the ink in his pen dried up. He threw it in the wastebasket and quickly grabbed a new pen from the desk drawer, continuing to write out his verses excitedly. But the empty pen said with sadness, "You could have filled me and used me again, but you preferred to throw me in the trash and get another pen to satisfy your narcissistic arrogance … You have forgotten how many poems I wrote for you … and how many important names and appointments that couldn't be put off I noted down for you from the kindness of my heart."

The pen fell into a burning silence and began to cry tears unknown to humanity, filling the wastebasket, while the poet composed his poem with unprecedented enthusiasm.

Enemies

I READ IN a book the following piece of wisdom: "Man is the enemy of what he doesn't know." When I traveled through the regions of the world, I saw in every place the enmity of man to man.

The Ship

WHEN I BECAME a third-class passenger on the ship of existence, I realized that I was very close to the engine of life.

The Teeth of the Comb

SOME OF THE teeth of the comb were envious of human class differences. They strived desperately to increase their height, and, when they succeeded, began to look with disdain on their colleagues below.

After a little while, the comb's owner felt a desire to comb his hair. But when he found it in this state, he threw it in the garbage.

We Won't Surrender

THE CURRENT OF the river spoke to the salmon who wouldn't stop going against him, saying, "Your stubbornness won't help you!"

But the fish answered him in one voice, "We won't surrender!"

Index of Titles

New Directions Paperbooks — a partial listing

Martín Adán, The Cardboard House
César Aira, Ema, the Captive
  An Episode in the Life of a Landscape Painter
  Ghosts
Will Alexander, The Sri Lankan Loxodrome
Paul Auster, The Red Notebook
Honoré de Balzac, Colonel Chabert
Djuna Barnes, Nightwood
Charles Baudelaire, The Flowers of Evil*
Bei Dao, City Gate, Open Up
Nina Berberova, The Ladies From St. Petersburg
Max Blecher, Adventures in Immediate Irreality
Roberto Bolaño, By Night in Chile
  Distant Star
  Last Evenings on Earth
  Nazi Literature in the Americas
Jorge Luis Borges, Labyrinths
  Professor Borges
  Seven Nights
Coral Bracho, Firefly Under the Tongue*
Kamau Brathwaite, Ancestors
Basil Bunting, Complete Poems
Anne Carson, Antigonick
  Glass, Irony & God
Horacio Castellanos Moya, Senselessness
Louis-Ferdinand Céline
  Death on the Installment Plan
  Journey to the End of the Night
Rafael Chirbes, On the Edge
Inger Christensen, alphabet
Jean Cocteau, The Holy Terrors
Peter Cole, The Invention of Influence
Julio Cortázar, Cronopios & Famas
Albert Cossery, The Colors of Infamy
Robert Creeley, If I Were Writing This
Guy Davenport, 7 Greeks
Osamu Dazai, No Longer Human
H. D., Tribute to Freud
  Trilogy
Helen DeWitt, The Last Samurai
Robert Duncan, Selected Poems
Eça de Queirós, The Maias
William Empson, 7 Types of Ambiguity
Shusaku Endo, Deep River
Jenny Erpenbeck, The End of Days
  Visitation
Lawrence Ferlinghetti
  A Coney Island of the Mind

F. Scott Fitzgerald, The Crack-Up
  On Booze
Forrest Gander, The Trace
Henry Green, Pack My Bag
Allen Grossman, Descartes' Loneliness
John Hawkes, Travesty
Felisberto Hernández, Piano Stories
Hermann Hesse, Siddhartha
Takashi Hiraide, The Guest Cat
Yoel Hoffman, Moods
Susan Howe, My Emily Dickinson
  That This
Bohumil Hrabal, I Served the King of England
Sonallah Ibrahim, That Smell
Christopher Isherwood, The Berlin Stories
Fleur Jaeggy, Sweet Days of Discipline
Alfred Jarry, Ubu Roi
B. S. Johnson, House Mother Normal
James Joyce, Stephen Hero
Franz Kafka, Amerika: The Man Who Disappeared
John Keene, Counternarratives
Laszlo Krasznahorkai, Satantango
  The Melancholy of Resistance
  Seiobo There Below
Eka Kurniawan, Beauty Is a Wound
Rachel Kushner, The Strange Case of Rachel K
Mme. de Lafayette, The Princess of Clèves
Lautréamont, Maldoror
Sylvia Legris, The Hideous Hidden
Denise Levertov, Selected Poems
Li Po, Selected Poems
Clarice Lispector, The Hour of the Star
  Near to the Wild Heart
  The Passion According to G. H.
Federico García Lorca, Selected Poems*
  Three Tragedies
Nathaniel Mackey, Splay Anthem
Stéphane Mallarmé, Selected Poetry and Prose*
Norman Manea, Captives
Javier Marías, Your Face Tomorrow (3 volumes)
Bernadette Mayer, Works & Days
Thomas Merton, New Seeds of Contemplation
  The Way of Chuang Tzu
Henri Michaux, Selected Writings
Dunya Mikhail, The War Works Hard
Henry Miller, The Colossus of Maroussi
  Big Sur & The Oranges of Hieronymus Bosch

Yukio Mishima, Confessions of a Mask
  Death in Midsummer
Eugenio Montale, Selected Poems*
Vladimir Nabokov, Laughter in the Dark
  Nikolai Gogol
  The Real Life of Sebastian Knight
Raduan Nassar, A Cup of Rage
Pablo Neruda, The Captain's Verses*
  Love Poems*
  Residence on Earth*
Charles Olson, Selected Writings
George Oppen, New Collected Poems
Wilfred Owen, Collected Poems
Michael Palmer, The Laughter of the Sphinx
Nicanor Parra, Antipoems*
Boris Pasternak, Safe Conduct
Kenneth Patchen
  Memoirs of a Shy Pornographer
Octavio Paz, Selected Poems
  A Tale of Two Gardens
Victor Pelevin, Omon Ra
Saint-John Perse, Selected Poems
René Philoctete, Massacre River
Ezra Pound, The Cantos
  New Selected Poems and Translations
Raymond Queneau, Exercises in Style
Qian Zhongshu, Fortress Besieged
Raja Rao, Kanthapura
Herbert Read, The Green Child
Kenneth Rexroth, Selected Poems
Keith Ridgway, Hawthorn & Child
Rainer Maria Rilke
  Poems from the Book of Hours
Arthur Rimbaud, Illuminations*
  A Season in Hell and The Drunken Boat*
Guillermo Rosales, The Halfway House
Evelio Rosero, The Armies
Fran Ross, Oreo
Joseph Roth, The Emperor's Tomb
  The Hundred Days
  The Hotel Years
Raymond Roussel, Locus Solus
Ihara Saikaku, The Life of an Amorous Woman
Nathalie Sarraute, Tropisms
Albertine Sarrazin, Astragal
Jean-Paul Sartre, Nausea
  The Wall
Delmore Schwartz
  In Dreams Begin Responsibilities

W.G. Sebald, The Emigrants
  The Rings of Saturn
  Vertigo
Aharon Shabtai, J'accuse
Hasan Shah, The Dancing Girl
C. H. Sisson, Selected Poems
Stevie Smith, Best Poems
Gary Snyder, Turtle Island
Muriel Spark, The Driver's Seat
  The Girls of Slender Means
  Memento Mori
George Steiner, My Unwritten Books
Antonio Tabucchi, Indian Nocturne
  Pereira Maintains
Junichiro Tanizaki, A Cat, a Man & Two Women
Yoko Tawada, Memoirs of a Polar Bear
Dylan Thomas, A Child's Christmas in Wales
  Collected Poems
  Under Milk Wood
Uwe Timm, The Invention of Curried Sausage
Charles Tomlinson, Selected Poems
Tomas Tranströmer
  The Great Enigma: New Collected Poems
Leonid Tsypkin, Summer in Baden-Baden
Tu Fu, Selected Poems
Frederic Tuten, The Adventures of Mao
Regina Ullmann, The Country Road
Jane Unrue, Love Hotel
Paul Valéry, Selected Writings
Enrique Vila-Matas, Bartleby & Co.
  Vampire in Love
Elio Vittorini, Conversations in Sicily
Rosmarie Waldrop, Gap Gardening
Robert Walser, The Assistant
  Microscripts
  The Tanners
Wang An-Shih, The Late Poems
Eliot Weinberger, The Ghosts of Birds
Nathanael West, The Day of the Locust
  Miss Lonelyhearts
Tennessee Williams, Cat on a Hot Tin Roof
  The Glass Menagerie
  A Streetcar Named Desire
William Carlos Williams, In the American Grain
  Selected Poems
  Spring and All
Mushtaq Ahmed Yousufi, Mirages of the Mind
Louis Zukofsky, "A"
  Anew

*BILINGUAL EDITION

For a complete listing, request a free catalog from New Directions, 80 8th Avenue, New York, NY 10011
or visit us online at ndbooks.com